For Tess,
who quite often stands alone
—J. O. B.

Copyright © 2000 by John O'Brien
All rights reserved

Published by Caroline House
Boyds Mills Press, Inc.
A Highlights Company
815 Church Street
Honesdale, Pennsylvania 18431
Printed in China

First edition, 2000
The text of this book is set in 30-point Caslon Roman.
The illustrations are done in watercolor and ink.
10 9 8 7 6 5 4 3 2 1

Publisher Cataloging-in-Publication Data

O'Brien, John.
    The farmer in the dell / illustrated by John O'Brien. 1st ed.
[32]p. : col. ill. ;   cm.
Summary: A humorously illustrated version of the traditional children's rhyme.
ISBN 1-56397-775-3
1. Nursery rhymes, American. 2. Children's poetry, American.
3. Folk songs, English — United States — Texts. [1. Nursery rhymes. 2. Folk songs — United
States. 3. Singing games. 4. Games.] I. Title.
782.42162/ 13 —dc21 2000 AC   CIP
99-60396

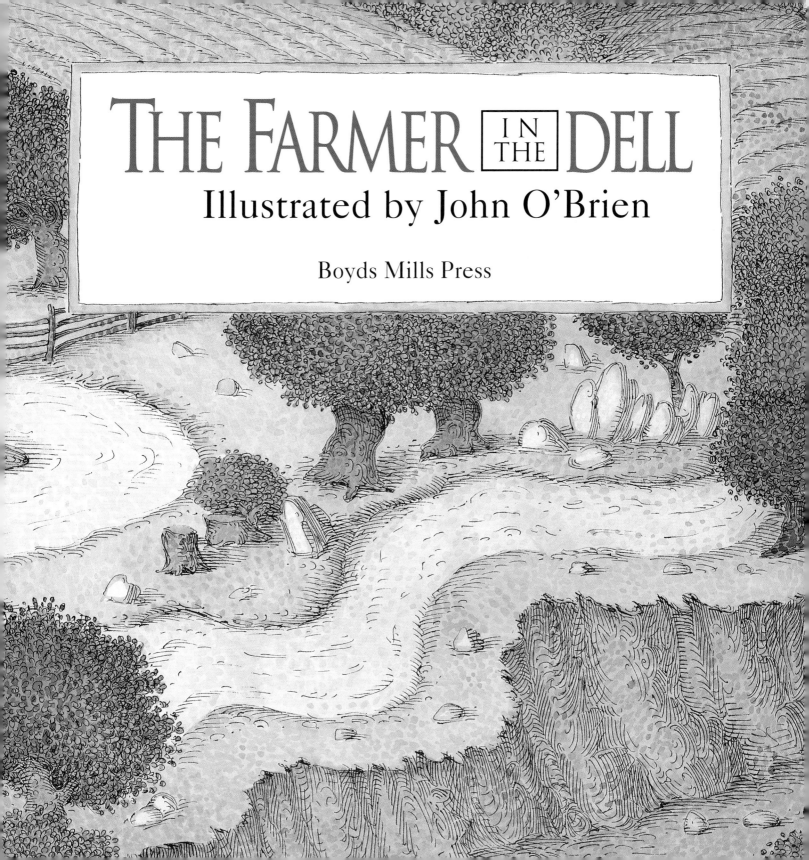

THE FARMER IN THE DELL

Illustrated by John O'Brien

Boyds Mills Press

THE FARMER . . .

. . . IN THE DELL,

The farmer in the dell,

Hi-ho, the derry-o!
The farmer in the dell.

The farmer takes a wife,
The farmer takes a wife,

Hi-ho, the derry-o!
The farmer takes a wife.

The wife takes a nurse,
The wife takes a nurse,

Hi-ho, the derry-o!
The wife takes a nurse.

The nurse takes a child,
The nurse takes a child,
Hi-ho, the derry-o!
The nurse takes a child.

The child takes a dog,
The child takes a dog,

Hi-ho, the derry-o!
The child takes a dog.

The dog takes a cat,
The dog takes a cat,

Hi-ho, the derry-o!
The dog takes a cat.

The cat takes a rat,
The cat takes a rat,

Hi-ho, the derry-o!
The cat takes a rat.

The cheese stands alone,

The cheese stands alone,

Hi-ho, the derry-o!

The cheese stands alone.

The rat takes the cheese,

The rat takes the cheese,

Hi-ho, the derry-o!

The rat takes the cheese.

The farmer . . .

. . . in the dell,

The farmer in the dell,
Hi-ho, the derry-o!
The farmer in the dell . . .